To my godson, Jonathan

Young Scott Books

Young Scott Books
by Mary Blount Christian

Nothing Much Happened Today
Devin and Goliath
No Dogs Allowed, Jonathan

Addison-Wesley Publishing Company, Inc.
Reading, Massachusetts 01867
Printed in the United States of America
Second Printing

WZ/WZ   6/75   01028

Library of Congress Cataloging in Publication Data

Christian, Mary Blount.
  No dogs allowed, Jonathan.
  SUMMARY: When Jonathan is finally successful in
smuggling a huge sheep dog into his apartment building,
he learns why dogs are against the rules.
  [1. Dogs—Fiction] I. Madden, Don, 1927–   illus.
II. Title.
PZ7.C4528Nm   [E]   74–2128
ISBN 0–201–01028–3

NO DOGS ALLOWED, JONATHAN!

By Mary Blount Christian

illustrated by Don Madden

Addison-Wesley

Thump. Thump. Thump.
Jonathan skidded to a stop.
''What's that?'' he asked aloud.
He heard panting.
''Who's there?'' he called into
the shadowy alley.

As Jonathan moved closer, a large pink tongue
rolled across his cheek. SLURP!
It was the shaggiest, biggest dog he'd ever seen.
A note tied to him read:
HIS NAME IS WOODROW.
PLEASE TAKE GOOD CARE OF HIM.
(SIGNED) EX-OWNER
Obediently Woodrow followed Jonathan to the
door of his apartment building.

"Hold it!" a voice boomed.
Humphrey, the doorman, scolded.
"You can't take that dog in there. It's against the rules."
"That's a dumb old rule," Jonathan replied grumpily.
"They let babies in, and dogs don't cry nearly so much."
Humphrey stood firmly between Jonathan and the door.
"Rules are rules. No dogs allowed," he said.
Woodrow left with Jonathan.

When Jonathan returned he was
pushing a baby buggy.
Humphrey smiled.
"Well, well. Taking little brother
for an outing. How nice."

The lump under the blanket moved. Thump.
Thump. Thump. Humphrey raised an eyebrow.
He jerked back the covers.
"It's that dog!" he shouted. "Rules are rules.
Out! Out!"

When Jonathan returned he was carrying a
lumpy laundry bag. Humphrey smiled. "Well,
well. You are helping your mother with the
laundry. How very nice."
Before Jonathan could protest, Humphrey picked
up the bag.
Slurp!
Humphrey sighed. "Jonathan. Your laundry
just *kissed* me."
"I know," Jonathan grumbled.
"Rules are rules. Out, out!"

Next Jonathan dressed Woodrow in his mother's blonde wig and her best skirt.

Then he disguised him as a teddy bear with a bright blue ribbon around his neck.

He even tried to make Woodrow look like a rocking horse.

But each time Humphrey stood firmly.

"Out, out, out!" he shouted.

At last while Humphrey was helping
Mrs. Dunkendorf with her groceries, Jonathan
and Woodrow sneaked into the apartment.

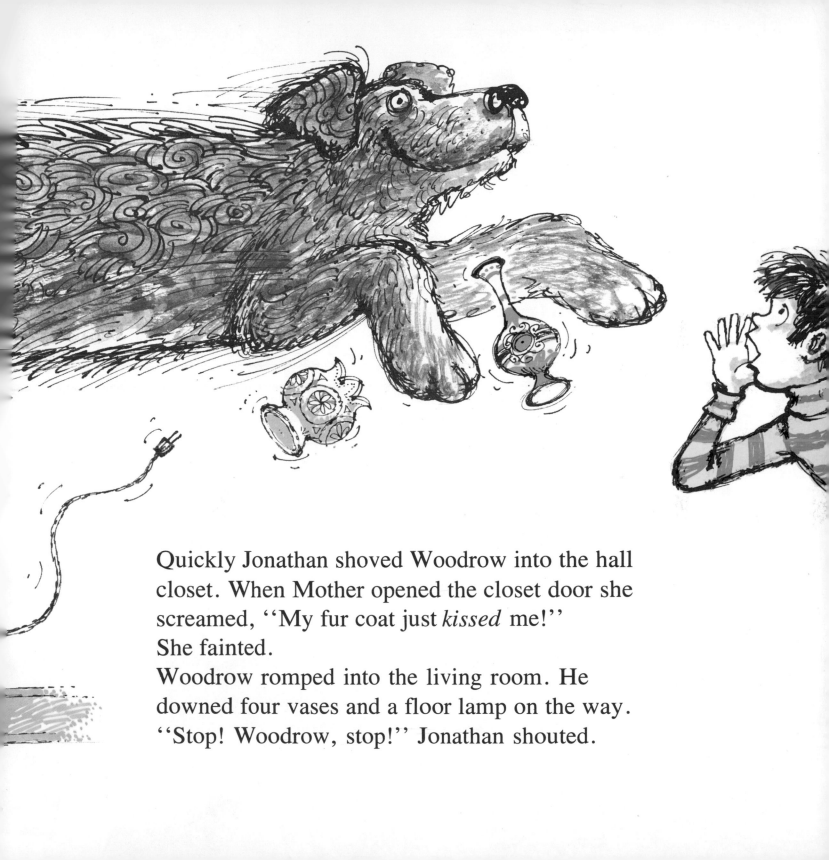

Quickly Jonathan shoved Woodrow into the hall closet. When Mother opened the closet door she screamed, "My fur coat just *kissed* me!"
She fainted.
Woodrow romped into the living room. He downed four vases and a floor lamp on the way.
"Stop! Woodrow, stop!" Jonathan shouted.

Woodrow jumped from the sofa to the coffee
table and back again, barking loudly.
Mother awakened and began shouting, ''There's
a giant bear in here! Help, help!''

The cook rushed in and began banging a pot with a big wooden spoon. "Shoo, bear! Shoo!" she shouted.

Humphrey ran in blowing his whistle. He shouted, "Out! Out! *Out!*"

Woodrow raced into the hall, landing on the scrub lady, who knocked a pail of sudsy water over the floor.

Woodrow skidded in the suds, landing on a potted philodendron.

Skidding through the suds immediately after that were Jonathan, Mother, the cook, and Humphrey, who was still blowing his whistle. They landed in a heap by Woodrow, who couldn't resist one good *slurp!* across Humphrey's soapy face.

Jonathan stared glassily at the line of frowning faces. He gazed unhappily at the path of broken glass, overturned furniture and suds. Managing a weak smile, he stammered, "So *this* is why no dogs are allowed."

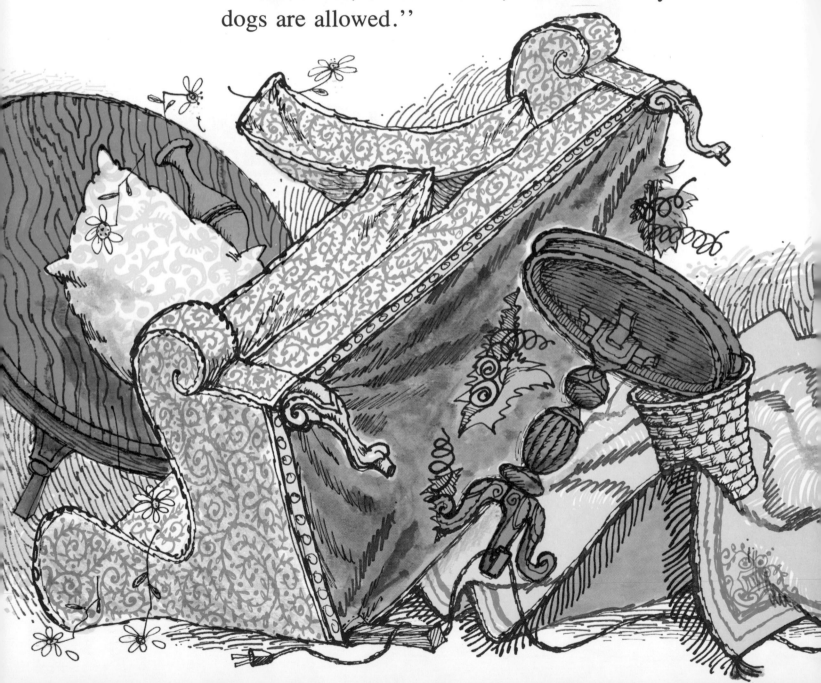

Woodrow's loudly thumping tail reminded Jonathan.
"But what about *him?*" Jonathan wailed.
Humphrey shrugged. "We could call the dog
catcher, I suppose."
"Nooooo," Jonathan begged. "*Not that*,
please! If I clean up all of this mess, and if
I promise to keep Woodrow on a leash, do you
think . . ."
But four heads shook *no* before he could finish.
A tear trickled down Jonathan's cheek.

"If I can't have him, maybe one of you . . ."
Again the heads shook no.
Woodrow rolled his pink tongue over
Humphrey's hand. His tail made a steady
thump, thump.
Jonathan beamed. "Look, Humphrey. He likes
you. *Almost* as much as he likes *me*."
Humphrey shrugged.
"Do you have a house, Humphrey?" Jonathan
asked hopefully.
"Yes."
"And a yard?"
"Yes."
"With a fence?"
Humphrey's netted eyebrows shot upward.
"Well, yes. I have a fence," he mumbled
helplessly. "But."
Jonathan grinned broadly. "Then *you* take
Woodrow!"

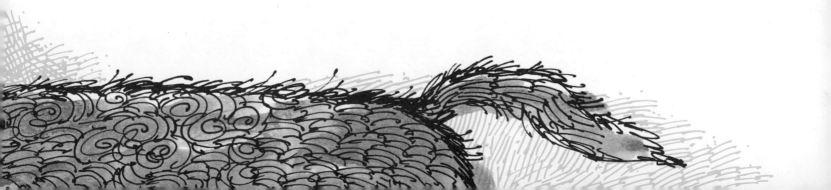

Humphrey's eyebrows netted again. ''But I don't really *need* . . .''

''Sure you do,'' Jonathan argued boldly. ''He could watch *your* door while you are watching *ours*.''

Humphrey smiled slightly.

''And,'' Jonathan continued while Humphrey was off guard. ''And it's not like you'd really *own* him. I would. All *you* need to do is give him a home.''

Humphrey looked puzzled.

''I could give him all the loving and brushing and things like that,'' Jonathan concluded. ''We could be *partners*.''

Woodrow whimpered and nuzzled his cold nose into Humphrey's hand. His eyes twinkling, Humphrey said, ''OK, Partner. I'm convinced.''

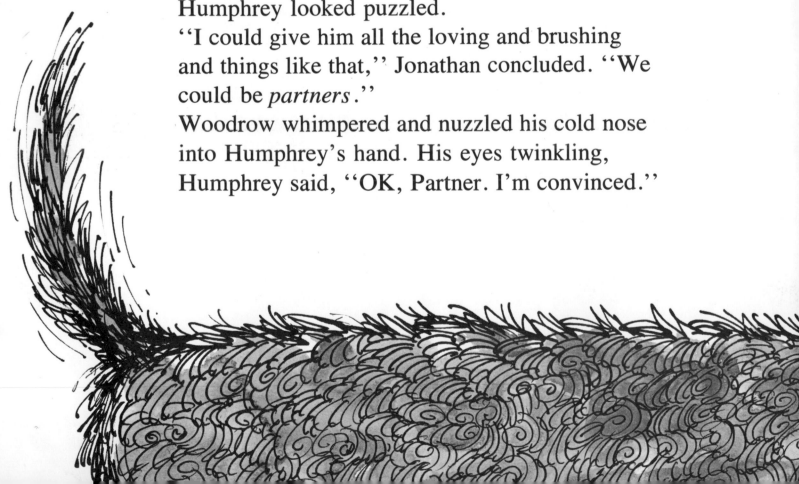

"Just one thing," Humphrey warned. "He has got to be *your* dog, not mine. Don't expect *me* to do any of the loving."

Humphrey winked broadly at the suds-covered spectators. They laughed happily. Woodrow kissed Jonathan, then Humphrey, then Jonathan again.

And his tail wagged a steady thump, thump, thump.